Tradition demands
The Doom of Change be spoken,
Else that stands shall fall,
That built is demolished,
Law falters and fails man,
And decay consumes all.
This is the doom.

Swans Over the Moon

Swans Over the Moon

A Novel

by Forrest Aguirre

Wheatland Press

Swans Over the Moon

Wheatland Press
P. O. Box 1818
Wilsonville, OR 97070

Library of Congress Cataloging-in-Publication data is
available upon request.
ISBN 978-0-9794054-0-2
Printed in the United States of America
Layout and cover design by Deborah Layne.

➤ One ⬥

The Judicar stood in the middle of his chambers, chin up, his thick arms extending straight out from the velvet robes that draped his substantial frame. He waited patiently as his two-headed servant lowered a breastplate over his head. The chromium-embossed scene of two majestic swans entwined in mid-flight combat over the cratered surface of the moon passed beneath his bearded chin to rest on his broad chest.

The servant next dressed his master's legs and solidly-grounded feet in greaves and sabaton. The ruler looked down with limpid blue eyes to the engravings etched into his armor. His irises reflected scintillating scenes as detailed as those painted on the three walls of the chamber in which he stood. Baroque scenes of conquest, ritual, and monumental architecture—built in celebration of the kingdom's glorious history and accomplishment—flowed from one wall to another, save on the side of the room to the nobleman's back. Behind him stood four immense white marble pillars, behind which a complex series of marble-floored hallways and doorways sprawled. Pygmies with eyelids sewn shut (lest their unworthy sight bear witness to the glory of the Judicar, whose palace this was), ran to and fro through the maze of rooms and halls, fulfilling errands and orders with pattering feet through a percussion ensemble of opening and slamming doors. All seemed in a rush, an emergency, bodies frantic at the behest of the royal bureaucracy. Occasionally, one of the slaves would crawl into the chamber on his knees, offering up another piece of the exquisitely-worked armor to the Judicar's two-headed servant, then, with bowed head, the dwarf would slide back on his knees to exit the chamber.

The Judicar was pensive. "Who say men that I am, Heterodymus?" Heterodymus' shriveled, lich-like left head answered first: "Men say that you are mad, that you should vacate the throne and let the people rule over their own interests," it croaked in a high, scratchy voice.

He nodded, thinking for a moment, then turned to the other head. "Dexter?" he asked, seemingly unaffected by the brashness of the left-head's comment.

The right head responded in a cool, reassuring voice whose cheerful tone contradicted the left head's as much as the godlike innocent beauty of his own baby face opposed the other's extreme ugliness. "Sinistrum is mistaken. Men say that you are the greatest ruler Procellarium has ever known. A genius in trade and tactics, my lord."

The Judicar weighed their words for a moment. "Madman or genius," the noble spoke in a dignified manner, without a hint of boasting or over-confidence, "I am their leader. Judicar Parmour Pelevin. And I will uphold the traditions of my people."

"Yes, my lord," Heterodymus' two heads spoke in unison, bowing to their liege.

"I'll vote for genius," a female voice, soft as a distant mountain breeze, declared from between the pillars behind the Judicar.

He turned, smiled. "Selene. My only comfort. How dare you flatter me?" he joked. "Come in, my dear."

She entered the room, gliding over the floor as if the ground itself retreated from her touch in obesiance to her standing as the Judicar's daughter. Her waist-length ghost-white hair flowed only slightly behind her crimson robes. Above her floated two apparitions—Tarans, those wispy souls of unbaptized infants that are often seen flitting about in cemeteries or dark woods, bewailing in mewing voices their terrible fates. But these two were quite contented, continually re-arranging a series of red silk scarves around the maiden's head, shoulders, waist, and arms, she simultaneously swelling and retreating, like a beating heart, as she approached.

Her lips hardly moved when she spoke, and the Judicar, who concentrated his sight through the ever-moving veils and scarves, thought that her full red lips never moved at all. Of course this must all be illusion, he assured himself. Selene's voice, faint as a whisper, projected forth with a soothing, yet piercing clarity. "And how can a daughter over-flatter her father, even if he is the Judicar?"

"There you go again, little swan. And what is it you wish from me at such an important hour, my young one?"

"Only to wish you good fortune". She handed him a crystal flask containing a phosphorescent golden liquid. "And to present you a gift in preparation for the upcoming engagement."

He looked at the flask, then to Selene. "My thanks. You are indeed, reason for good cheer. You brace my confidence."

She curtsied, smiling, the Tarans lowering and rising with her, as if on tethers. With a slight nod, she turned to glide between the pillars and into the maze of halls and doors, sightless pygmies parting before her like fog before sunlight, so powerfully was her presence felt.

"And now," he said to himself as he watched her leave, his smile fading with her departure, "it is time." He turned his back to the pillars as Selene disappeared through a distant doorway. A wrinkle of determination fixed itself to his brow. He breathed in deeply, then exhaled slowly through his aqualine nose, steeling himself to face some enemy.

"Sinistrum, begin the recounting" the Judicar spoke. Heterodymus' left head raised its slit-like eyelids to reveal yellowed orbs buried beneath manifold layers of wrinkled flesh. "Recite to me The Doom of Change."

Sinistrum spoke slowly, deliberately. Apprehension pricked the back of his parched and withered throat:

Tradition demands
The Doom of Change be spoken,
Else that stands shall fall,
That built is demolished,
Law falters and fails man,
And decay consumes all.
This is the doom.

The right head spoke next, its features evincing an articulation at odds with their infantile appearance, its voice a sing-song entirely inappropriate for the gravity of the circumstance in which it spoke. "Sinistrum speaks rightly, my lord. It is so."

"Now, Dexter. Explain the carvings on this ailette," the Judicar tapped his left shoulder piece beneath the war-blade that jutted out like a shredding-saw from his rotator cuff. It showed a pillar, cracked in half, falling over onto a single rose that grew up out of the lunar soil. Behind the pillar, shoving the column over in the direction of the flower, stood the naked figure of the Judicar, his long, curly hair cascading over the taut sinews of his neck and shoulders.

The servant's baby head let out a long, high-pitched sigh. He lowered his sight to the floor. Dexter did not want to say what was required of him.

Nevertheless, duty over-rode desire, and he spoke while fastening the Judicar's mail and leather armbands and gauntlets over his velvet sleeves and lace cuffs. "This is the consequence of ignoring The Doom of Change. One Judicar defied The Doom, missing the required ambulation of the Krieger pools. At the Hour of Ambulation, this Judicar and his wife bathed at the palace, putting the pleasures of the flesh above the order of the kingdom. They exited the bath, but when the gongs of deep midnight sounded, at the exact moment when the ambulation should have ended, a pillar cracked free from its footing, falling and crushing the life-breath from the Judicar's wife."

"And who was this Judicar?" Pelevin asked in a stern, yet trembling voice, impatient for an answer.

Dexter's head lowered, silent.

"It is you, my lord," Sinistrum answered. He handed the Judicar his ornately-carved blunderbuss pistol, then fastened the warrior-ruler's rapier around the Judicar's waist.

"And that," the armed and armored Judicar Parmour Pelevin stated, as he turned towards the pillars of his palace and the labyrinthine halls that lay beyond, "is why I go now to kill my daughter, Selene's sister, the ever-wayward and increasingly unpredictable Cimbri Pelevin. She will not see the next star-rise. Prepare my steed. Ready my men. We ride."

The Judicar quaffed the contents of the crystal flask given to him earlier by Selene—nepenthe and absinthe to nullify the pain of the past and bolster his courage for the forthcoming engagement. He threw the flask to the floor in resignation, causing it to explode into a hundred shards, then strode out into the hallway, blind pygmies scattering before him like sheep before a wolf, only to gather behind him picking up the glassy slivers left in his wake. Their knees and fingers bled on the armory's floor, beneath the swans of the moon.

⇒ Two ⇐

On a high, white bluff overlooking a vast lunar flat land, Selene Pelevin sat in a wicker chair under a large pink parasol. A cadre of pygmies attended the young noble-woman and the two hundred other women and girls similarly positioned atop the cliff. Some served the women tea and biscuits, others waved palm fronds to keep the moon dust from soiling the ladies' lily-white silks. The servants were as busy as the women were sedentary.

Selene, like the other women, wore a billowing white dress altogether too large for her slim frame, which gave her the appearance of a pulsating albino queen-ant whenever a breeze blew. Her Tarans entertained themselves by playfully winding and unwinding her scarves around her head and arms as she sipped tea, a bloated insect-puppet on strings, two infantile puppeteers dancing in the air above the pom-

pom fringed umbrella.

The other women also wore voluminous dresses and brimmed hats adorned with flower blossoms. They spoke of past battles and the Knights of Procellarium's bravery, how the pale-blue-skinned savages of Wollaston had fled before the glistening blades of the Judicar's guard chittering in their insectoid tongue as they were crushed into submission under hoof and steel. Between war tales, they gossiped about theater and fashion, their gardens and hobbies, and how good help was so difficult to come by. The sound of hooves from the valley below interrupted their whispers and giggles. A hush blanketed the women, and their pygmy servants produced small brass telescopes and mother-of-pear-inlaid opera glasses from wooden boxes, proffering them to their ladies. Hundreds of lenses soon glittered with miniature reflections of the plains below, all moving in one sweep, like a giant cliff-side kaleidoscope.

The southern rim of the Rüinker Plateau was cut by a line of mounted riders 100 wide. Silver potiels adorned the horse's heaving breasts, reflecting a hint of blue from the immense planet that nearly filled the dark sky above the soon-to-be battlefield. Mail twinkled and shimmered from beneath the saddles, giving the thin line a blue-white iridescence in the dark of night. The Judicar and his Procellarian knights appeared to ride on a glowing wave of hooves as they crossed that once-fertile plain, laid desolate, along with the rest of the moon some millenia ago by industrialization, massive over-farming, and environmental reckless-ness. Perhaps, in time, mankind might reach outward to that planet that glowed blue and green, as the moon once had, not with mere crater-pockets of bare subsistence, but with throbbing life. But in the meantime, the decrees of conservation were all that the Judicar and his people could cling to. All else was a continuation of decay, the fulfillment of decrepitude. Every-thing has its equal and opposite reaction, the Procellarian scientists had found, and the Procellarian nation stood to oppose entropy by embodying and enforcing order. In time, they concluded, law would prevail.

The Judicar held his gauntleted hand up to the square, commanding his army to halt. The smell of horse foam and sweat caught up with the men, settling into their nostrils as they awaited their orders. The discomfort and stench, not to mention the distraction of their wives and daughters spectating from an overlooking bluff, added to their unease.

After sending out a squad of vedettes for

reconnaissance, the Judicar beckoned Hetero-dymus to his side. Then, having raised a long brass spyglass to his eyes, he dictated to his two-headed assistant, Dexter nodding, looking at the scroll on which he wrote while Sinistrum squinted, looking at the northern horizon where a black mass marched toward them, a low cloud of dust in its wake.

The Judicar spoke slowly and deliberately:

"In the star-illumined twilight I could see them marching in a firing-line across the plateau, several hundred strong. It was difficult to judge their exact numbers because of the manner in which their shadows fell on each other, like blackened match sticks constantly re-arranging themselves in an ever-tightening box as their amoebic mass assumed fighting formation. An ebony army of marionettes. Everything about them was long and thin, from their proboscopic-nosed ivory masks to their black top hats, some four feet high, to the razor-thin, single elongated slits in their masks that served somehow as eyeholes. Even their weapons, wide-butted flintlock muskets with barrels the length of a man and more, bespoke aphotic darkness thrusting like a knife into light. That gaunt army bristled like a penumbric nest of stilettos. We stood ready to quench the dark fires of the Scaramouche, like our fathers before us."

Heterodymus put his stylus away, Dexter looking up at the Judicar with an expression of awe, while Sinistrum continued to assess the enemy's strength. "It is a worthy account, M'lord," Dexter declared with great admiration. Sinistrum nodded, grunting his assent, not taking his eyes off the approaching army.

"Now the record is your keep," the Judicar nodded to Dexter. "I ride, for duty demands it." He spurred his horse forward.

The Judicar broke from the line, galloping across the monochromatic wasteland. At a carfax halfway between the two armies, he halted and dismounted, inviting the enemy to parlay with a shouted challenge.

"Forth, coward! We, the invictive, bring desolation to your lands, unless you surrender forthwith."

The black box pulsed, as if preparing to burst, ejecting some foreign object from its mass. Finally, when the anfractuous gyrations of the formation bulged at the front, a breach appeared, revealing the onrushing figure of a young woman, black hair whipping behind her tightly-muscled body as she sprinted toward the carfax, a bird of prey on the hunt, arms held out for balance. She stopped suddenly still, only two footsteps from the Judicar's stone face. She stood glowering, as tall as the Judicar in her ankle-length vermillion gambeson, a bright red star in the blackness. A thin basket-hilt rapier hung from her belt, but her main weapon was the same as that of her troops, a long-barreled flintlock affixed with a long, thin stinger of a black bayonet. She looked up at the blade, slowly tracing the blood groove down towards the stock with a long finger, admiring the utility of the weapon. Finally, she focused her attention on the Judicar.

"Father," a defiant acknowledgement, grudging in its tone.

"Cimbri." His voice lacked emotion.

"Come for the ritual slaughter, I see."

"I tried to burke your treason. A demarche was sent."

"A demarche meant to expire this night, whether heeded or not. And your challenge," she sneered, "is, of course, without honor. Surrender? So that your noble knights can fall on the Scaramouche without the fuss of a fight? That is not nobility. That is genocide."

"It is our praxis."

"No," she breathed in through her nose, trying to contain her anger, though her disdain was clearly evident, "it is yours alone. I reject it, in the name of my noble mother."

"Your mother is dead, girl, as you soon will be, unless you surrender."

"I cannot surrender. Mother would not approve," she said, seething venom.

"Damn you, silly girl!" he shouted so loudly that the echoes of his words stopped only just short of the spectator-women's ears. His knights chuckled uneasily. "Renounce your disloyalty, reject your insolence, and you shall live."

"Disloyalty to whom? To you? Your office? Your dedication to the outdated traditions that put you in this despicable situation in the first place?"

"I have put myself in the hands of our praxis to preserve my people."

"And what of the people who die as a result? What do you care for them?"

It was his turn to sneer. "What other people?"

She looked over her shoulder at the army behind her, then turned her searing gaze back to him. "You see in the Scaramouche only long-nosed ebony masks, empty eye pits. You see them as inferior creatures, mere beasts whose only worth is to suffer at your hands. You fail to understand them, therefore you despise them. I see a race of beauty, a people of rich cultural heritage, individuals with dreams and loves and passions and families; a people who, every year at this appointed time—your appointed time, not theirs—are subjected to the raids of your kin and kingdom, not because they pose any real threat to Procellarium, but because stale tradition dictates this course. A curse on your pestiferous praxis!"

He spat his response: "I see an ancient pestilence of creatures birthed from the blackest crater mouths of the dark side, spewing forth like black rivers toward my kingdom for generations untold. And now," he stood erect, slowing his speech to emphasize his words, "at their head I see a traitor to the kingdom of her birth, to her father, to her people, and to the very memory of the mother that brought her to life."

Cimbri's brow creased with rage, her scowling face approaching the crimson hue of her armor. She wheeled from the Judicar and bolted back to her troops, disappearing in their midst.

The Judicar mounted his horse and galloped back to the line. The earth cast barely-visible blue rays over the rock-littered plateau, filling the widening void between them with a ghostly curtain of light.

Heterodymus climbed the ramp, which was worn from centuries of use as an approach to the highest observation point overlooking the Rüinker Plateau – the apex of the bluff from which seven dynasties of generals had laid their battle plans and waged their wars. The ectoplasmic remains of countless officers and soldiers eddied in the dust as he slowly scaled the steep slope. The curve of the ramp ended in a straight ridge, like a lizard's tail leading up to the spine, on which the observers sat, though the women and girls who had come to watch the scene knew little of the weighty decisions that had been made from this point in the past, the ebb and flow of empires that commenced and ended right there. From this historic point the Judicar's advisor would observe the coming battle.

He negotiated the steamer trunks and portable tea pantries that stood hidden behind the women's parasols, careful not to interrupt a pair of pygmies who were playing chess with stylized Scara-mouche and Procellarian Knight pieces. A group of some dozen or more servant spectators listened with great interest as the opening moves were called out:

b2-b4

g7-g5

Heterodymus walked around them, the sounds of the contestants' declarations growing fainter, but still a part of the background noise. He then stepped through the umbrellas and into Selene's sitting area. Her Tarans gave a start as he surprised them with his sudden appearance. They flitted quickly up and away, nearly choking the young lady with her own scarf. Heterodymus stifled a giggle as she shot bolt upright.

"What!?" she shrieked, a command as much as a question.

"Many pardons, M'lady. I think I may have given your . . . your . . . young ones a bit of a startle," Dexter said softly, his sarcasm as subtle as his voice. Sinistrum followed, his grating voice in utter contrast to Dexter's sonorous tones. "Beg pardon, Madame." He bowed.

She looked up cautiously to see the disposition of her Tarans. "My pets, are you well?" she said in a sickly sweet voice. "Oh, my babies. The ugly man won't hurt you, my pets." They cooed their lamentable best.

Satisfied, she took up her opera glasses and turned her attention to the battlefield below.

"I see that the Queen of the Savages has entered into negotiations," she said disinterestedly. "Perhaps she will surrender, though that would be a bit of a shame."

"A shame?" Sinistrum almost snarled. "Surrender would spare her life, young lady Selene. There is no shame in it."

"Let us not speak of age. Even the oldest may

prove the most unwise, counselor of the Judicar. Senility comes to the aged, not the young." A few nearby women giggled at her cutting remarks. Sinistrum glared at her.

Dexter spoke, the Tarans looking at him jealously, frustrated that they were unable to express themselves verbally, as he could, despite the chronological similarity of their visages. "My apologies, Lady Selene. I only thought that you might be concerned with the ultimate outcome of your sister's decision."

"And why should I?" she sneered.

The heads looked at each other with combined perplexity and disgust, unable to decide between them whether to be outraged at her callousness, or merely to pity her lack of compassion. "My brother," Sinistrum spoke carefully, "is blood of my blood. I should not want to see him come to harm, under any circumstance. Our shared love…"

"You couldn't break from each other if you wanted to," Selene interrupted, the gaggle of women snickering again, "Whereas all my sister and I share now is our father. Besides, your emotions get in the way of proper administration. Cimbri has betrayed my father, whom I love. She is a traitor to both man and kingdom and thus must reap the consequences of her choices."

The other women along the line nodded their approval and whispered to one another in an aural wave expanding to either side of her, as if she were a stone pillar pushed over into a conversational pond, her pronouncements causing ripples in the social fabric of the nobility.

"Your father does not want to fight Lady Cimbri," Sinistrum crackled.

"He still loves her and remembers how she used to be," Dexter added.

"She used to be a monopolizer of her mother's time. Now she monopolizes my father's time with her meaningless entreaties. And where did she get that ridiculous outfit?" Laughter spread down the line. "Besides all that, the Judicar will do what he knows is right. He will behave responsibly for the kingdom and its people, unlike my rebellious sister."

"You seem to have been offended by her," Dexter said. Sinistrum was now glaring at the Tarans, trying, quite successfully, to scare them. They continued to rearrange scarves, but with a wary eye on the left head, sure to keep Selene between them and the ugly man.

"I think she was more offended by me," Selene said.

"No," Dexter said in mock sympathy, dripping

with sarcasm.

She was so wrapped up in her own thoughts and observations that she did not catch the mockery. "Yes. She never did care for me, more especially since mother died. It's plain to see that she is jealous of my relationship with our father. Of course, this may be the misplaced affection of an old maid who has never known a man. Some people wear their insecurities on their sleeve."

The two heads looked at each other with a sly grin. "There m'lady," they both said in cacophonic unison, "you speak nothing but the truth." Heterodymus turned away from Selene, his two-faced smile in contradiction with the mood of the battle unfolding on the plain below.

⇒ Three ⇐

The Scaramouche moved first, a slowly-marching rectangular formation spiked with extended weapons like a giant, sea urchin-encrusted barge crawling across the barren moonscape. The bustling ink-flow seethed with purpose in a cadence of stately progression, flowing over rocks and through dry wadis as the blue planet loomed ever larger up above.

Ten pairs of Procellarian vedettes galloped out to scout weaknesses and harass the enemy's flanks and rear. They rode in two lines, criss-crossing each other in "S" patterns across the dust of the Ruinker Plateau, forming wide, flat figure "8"s the breadth of the approaching formation. A volley smoked forth from the front of the black rectangle, dropping a dozen riders before they bore down on the soft flanks. The rider-less mounts of the slain meandered off to the northeast, no doubt fated to become meat for the multiple-legged, long-toothed denizens of Crater

Mairan and Mare Imbrium beyond, voids across which no sane man, at least none who wished to keep his reason, would dare to pass.

On the crest overlooking the battlefield, the pygmies continued their game:

White Nb5

Black xb5

The Judicar waited until he could hear the clang of his skirmishers' swords on Scaramouche equipment and the ricochet of enemy musket balls off of his soldiers' breast plates. Then, with the sound of metal on metal as his battle call, he bolted forward, leading the cavalry charge, nervous breath hissing through his gritted teeth. The Procellarian knights, four score strong, galloped forward toward the heart of the enemy formation, where they would attempt to carve their way back and out to meet the skirmishers that even now harangued the black army from the outside, thus cutting the enemy force into thirds.

Dust choked the air by the time the Judicar reached the first line of enemy troops, and it was only with great difficulty that he placed his first shot. His horse jostled underneath him, trampling the enemy under hoof. His blunderbuss pistol discharged point blank into the nearest Scaramouche's face, spattering mask, bone, and flesh in a mist of gore that coated his lap and right leg. He drew his rapier, slowly circling his horse to get a clear view of his surroundings above the fray, but the tourbillon was too great. He soon found himself in the midst of the enemy, completely surrounded. His horse buckled beneath him, its armor punctured by dozens of enemy bayonets. The weight of the animal's falling body crushed several Scaramouche troopers, their immense top hats flattened beneath the horse's mass. The collapse of the beast cleared an opening into which the Judicar tumbled as he flew from the saddle.

White Kxd5

His mind was awash in memorized ancestral epics wherein the Scaramouche were treated with scorn, a sort of clown-people who fled with whoops and silly dances when confronted by enemies with even the least bit of resolve. Surrounded, now, he wondered if the ghosts of those caricatured Scaramouche had returned to aid their descendants in turning the table of ridicule on the Procellarian monarch. He noted that they had never fought with such determination, usually breaking and fleeing even before the initial charge. This battle would long be remembered as the first great resistance of the Scaramouche. No matter, he thought, he had carried the day against more fearsome opponents under more compromised circumstances. They would win, of this the Judicar had no doubt. The only unsurety lay in the number of pages who would need to be knighted to fill the ranks of the fallen. The wailing of the Procellarian women would be insufferable, and the nobility would be sorely taxed to muster enough able youth into the army.

He carved a small space with his rapier, barely big enough to swing his sword. The dust cloud kicked up by the fall of his mount gave him enough reprieve to draw his poniard and fight two-handed, the way he preferred it. He heard, rather than saw, the battle – the diminishing rate of musket discharges to his rear, the echoes of ringing metal on metal, a scream from one of his troops far out on the left flank, the almost-silent fall of Scaramouche corpses before his sword and dagger – through this he created an aural map of the battlefield. Despite his success in melee (he had cut down at least five since his horse died, and taken as many with his falling steed), his knights were slowly losing to the Scaramouche's superior numbers. Doubt now began to prod at the edges of his thoughts, and he wondered if his confidence would begin to bleed out of him, assuring his defeat.

He thought he heard one of his knights nearby, a familiar voice among the chaos. He cut down two more of the enemy with one stroke on the way to his battle companion's voice. Too late did he realize that the voice screaming above the din belonged to no man, but to a woman, and that his foray had landed him even deeper in the midst of the enemy. Doubt was making inroads, and a tingling fear rose in his gullet. The battle pushed outward, away from him, like an expanding bubble. The growing void around him did nothing to embolden him, instead he felt naked and vulnerable. This apprehension to exposure scattered his battle focus so that he startled when he turned and saw Cimbri in the expanding circle. He knew then that it was her voice that had drawn him there.

White Ke5

Black Qe6

They spotted each other simultaneously and both were struck by the cosmic inevitability of their encounter here, alone, at the heart of the battle. They circled each other, looking for an opening to present itself, an opportunity to strike, she with a blood-encrusted bayonet, he with his rapier and poniard. The clatter of battle continued to recede from them, the shuffling of feet on dust and their breathing the only sounds to fill that eerie vacuum.

Cimbri had the demeanor of a crazed dog, hair standing out at odd angles, eyes agape, blood and saliva falling from her mouth. Every nerve aware and tingling with electricity. Bloodlust overtook her.

She used the length of her weapon to keep the Judicar at bay. He feinted with a downward thrust toward her legs, but she caught the deception, following through with a low strike, piercing his thigh deep into muscle tissue until she hit bone with the tip of the blade. She smiled a crazed smile, twisting the bayonet with a turn of her wrist and a grunt of effort, holding her weapon against the Judicar's leg bone, further emphasizing his vulnerability to her. But her face dropped quickly into despair as he took advantage of her gloating, hacking her strong hand off at the wrist with one swift slash in her momentarily glory-numbed second of inaction. She dropped to one knee as he slid his leg off the bayonet, the pain of extraction burning and pounding far more than the pain of the initial penetration. He limped over to where she knelt, transfixed with confusion, unable to steady her weapon while simultaneously gripping the stump of her wrist. She quickly put her free hand to her breasts, tearing out a frilly jabot and pressing it to the crimson-spilling wound to staunch the uncontrolled flow of blood.

The Judicar lowered the point of his sword to her neck, held her chin up with the weapon's blade. He looked into the eyes of the daughter he once loved.

In his peripheral vision he caught flashes of ivory on black through the dust, the muffled pattering of approaching footsteps drummed from somewhere beyond his sight. A warm gust of wind blew the wall of dust away and the Judicar looked around to find himself surrounded by Scaramouche, three dozen or so, their bayonets all pointed towards the familial pair, a fanged maw of steel about to sink teeth into its prey.

"Stalemate," he rasped.

"No," she conceded, "you have won. I will soon pass out from blood loss and they will flee, leaderless. You will, no doubt, rout their army and kill the weak and the stragglers. But before that, I want you to hear and understand." She shivered, and her breathing became erratic. Her eyes fluttered uncontrollably, though she strained hard to maintain control over herself.

"You have fought bravely. I will grant this request – as one warrior to another." Any hint of parental affection was lost in the formality of his voice.

She nodded and as she did a low moan sounded from the surrounding Scaramouche, a moan that rose and dipped, struck and eddied, wheeled into a plaintive, beautiful song.

The Judicar looked from side to side, fearful and perplexed, but saw that his enemy's bayonets no longer pointed at him. "What is this witchcraft?" he demanded with combined annoyance and fear, pushing her chin up again with his blade.

His daughter, nearly breathless with the effort it took to stay awake, replied. "Listen. You will recognize . . ."

He acquiesced for the honor of the oath. The hair on the back of his neck stood on end when he placed the haunting tune.

Images of his daughters and wife wheeled back in time, like a stack of daguerrotypes being flipped rapidly backwards from present to past by some invisible hand, the light of his memories fluttering like candlelight in their wind. The visions slowed, then stopped on a scene of his wife playing a harp, the blue of earthlight at night cascading through the glass roof above the royal bedchamber, oceans dripping liquid music from the instrument's strings. Her voice, warm and serene, almost filled their bedchamber, the cooing of a baby – Cimbri, and, years later, her younger sister Basia, then Selene. The room was filled with a fulsome warmth that created a sanctuary from the dying world on the cold lunar surface above the bedchamber.

The comfort of those most private moments filled him, momentarily. But the bedchamber evaporated before his eyes as nervousness, then a deep-welling anger flowed from him as he returned to the present, surrounded by Scaramouche singing this song, a song that only his wife could have known fully. "How," he questioned, his voice full of accusation, "how do they know this song? This was your mother's song."

"No," Cimbri cried, "It is their song, father. It tells of a mother's miraculous discovery that she could feed her child from her own breasts, that the child need not kill to eat until it grew, and the peace that entered childhood as a result of that discovery. It is one of their founding myths. I did not teach it to them."

"Then your mother," a searing revelation dawned on him, "your mother learned it from . . . them?"

A weak smile creased Cimbri's pallid face. "I see beauty. You see darkness. And in that darkness, mother hid this thing from you. She feared that you would not see their beauty as she and I did. I fear she was right."

The song slowed and the Scaramouche sauntered

northward just as the sound of hoof beats approached from the south. The Judicar's freshly-rallied troops crashed into the rear column of the retreating Scaramouche, breaking them into small pockets that gave little resistance to the slaughter inflicted on them. The hoofs of the Procellarian's horses became encrusted with a pink paste composed of the soil of a dying world mixed with the blood of a retreating army. The Judicar involuntarily fell to one knee and watched the waning battle paint the landscape in long streaks to the north.

The Procellarian knights cheered the rout, then helped their enfeebled commander onto the back of an abandoned steed. He rode back to the cliff and ascended with assistance, wounded, but un-defeated. Selene greeted him with a kiss and a glass of wine, which he drank deeply, not stopping until the vessel was empty and as dry as the plains to his back.

"Father," Selene said dramatically so that all would hear, a theatrical performance as much as a greeting. "Another victory for our people. Hurrah!"

The women and girls cheered him as his knights, working on the bleak plain below, constructed a gallows with the bones and muskets of the dead and dying Scaramouche. There the Judicar's traitorous daughter was hung for treason on the bodies of those she mistakenly loved, astride the weapons of sedition.

The Judicar, weakened by his wound, slumped down in Selene's chair and fell into blackness. His closing vision that night was the sight of Selene and the knight's women clapping and cheering to the death throes of his Cimbri. The Tarans floated up, Selene's long white scarf framing in a circle beneath them the last sight of that place. His daughter, Cimbri, a broken body swinging on the wind of the lunar night.

⟿ Four ⟿

The dead were buried, per Procellarian tradition, under mounds of white roses that were then ritually watered by the tears of the deceased's kin. The Judicar oversaw the ceremony, then led the knights back to the palace strapped to the saddle of a fallen knight's horse. The knight's family considered this the highest honor and walked alongside the steed, keeping their leader from sloughing off to the side from exhaustion.

The victory celebration was bittersweet with the loss of so many knights, but the survivors were drunk with their own successes long before they were drunk with wine. The Judicar gave a brief memoriam of the fallen men, a congratulations to the victors, and jokingly ordered all to have fun, on pain of death. But his façade of happiness could not last long, he knew, nor could he stand the pain of his wound and keep decorum, so he retired as soon as possible to his bedchamber.

Selene led her father from the banquet hall to his bedchamber, where she helped him remove his armor. She laid the individual pieces in an ancient velvet-lined chest, carefully arranging them in their proper order. He flopped down onto his throne with a grunt and sipped the healing tea that she had brought to him, watching the girl and noting how different she appeared, in both looks and mannerisms, from her mother. Perhaps her older sisters had taken the most from their mother, leaving her only the leftovers of the genetic inheritance. They were so different, in fact, that the Judicar found it difficult to keep the image of his wife and of Selene fixed in his mind at the same time, as if one would not allow the other his full attention.

She helped her father up from his arm chair. Pain shot through his leg, almost causing him to collapse, but he leaned on her for support. He noted, through his pain, how light, yet how powerful she was. She was thin and short, but her frame felt as if it were constructed of steel. Energy emanated from her like heat from a coal stove, whereas he felt, now, like a spent cinder. He noted also that the Tarans were careful to keep Selene between them and him. They cast wary glances at him as if expecting punishment at his hand for some misdeed. His leg throbbed, though, and soon all concern about the spirits was swallowed up in a sea of pain.

Selene guided him toward a side chamber, then left him with a kiss on the cheek, so that he might undress completely before entering the small, spherical hot bath room that adjoined the Judicar's bedchamber. Steam disgorged from its mouth like a steel forge at maximum capacity. He disrobed and hobbled up the stone stairway that led to the circular hatch opening. The smell of eucalyptus mingled with cinnamon and clove unguents – meant to cover the medicinal stench of pain-killers in the bath—flooded his head as he carefully lowered his wounded leg into the spiced water. He leaned back, closing the hatch with a spin of the wheeled handle, then sat down heavily in the narcotic water.

The entire inside of the sphere was carved in low-relief scenes in marble, studded with mosaic tiles. Above hovered the earth, the blue planet forever-present in the sky above Procellarium, a celestial sentinel eye, caught in eternal stasis on the ceiling. One half of the room showed stylized sun rays beating down, the other half falling stars, all showering down from the great orb of the sister planet. Midway round the chamber, in a thick band that ran the full inner circumference of the sphere, was a representation of Procellarium, palm trees and oases beneath crater lips, over which crystalline waterfalls spilled into spray. Pillars and arches thrust up through the vegetation, a sensual dance of flora and architecture. Birds and small animals, mostly lemurs and chameleons, moved from branch to branch, some even leaping up into the background of falling stars or sun rays above the buildings and trees. Beneath the band lay a stark landscape of bone-white desert plains and the gray, desolate mountains of the moon.

Lifeless.

Sterile.

Sepulchural.

Pallid.

Emaciated.

At the bottom of the sphere, beneath the blood-tinged churning bath water, lay a carving of a darkened crater, its gaping maw black and all-consuming, an abyss. Only now, these many years since he ascended his father's throne, did he begin to fear that darkness. He looked into it, and tunnel vision closed in on him, drawing his sight into the blackness, his consciousness into the pit.

From the midst of the void he heard a voice, distant and indistinct, yet familiar. Deep in the well a muted glittering cloud appeared from nothing at all and slowly coalesced into almost un-decipherable words. Beneath the words emerged a female figure, who voiced the words written in the darkness above her. The words and figure slowly became clearer, and though they remained difficult to see and hear, as if his ears were stuffed with cotton and his eyes blurred by sand, he recognized the voice and body as his wife's. He also knew the cadence of those words, burnt on his consciousness so long ago: their last conversation as they lay naked beneath a pillar, spent from lovemaking, lazily caressing each other's bodies. The rumble of rock sliding on rock, followed by the couple's mingled screaming, which grew more and more clear in the Judicar's ears, as if coming out of a tunnel or waking from a dream, immediately proceeded a shift in the image and in the voice.

The image changed from the darkened, barely-recognizable form of his wife to a clearer, lighter, yet still blurred image of Cimbri, as if she were surrounded in an illuminated mist. Her voice was clearer and seemed to emanate from an area in closer proximity to her body than had her mother's. The old words melted into new letters to reflect the words that Cimbri spoke: "And in the darkness, mother hid this thing from you. She feared that you would not see . . ."

And again the voice changed as the body and face metamorphosed, now into a vision of his second child, Basia. A faint aura shone around her, outlining her in a glowing light. But her beauty was twisted in anger, her blond tresses flailing in the blackness, a soft, glowing waterfall of gold disturbed by the vigorous action of her shaking head and the wide hand gestures indicating negation. Again, the words formed from the detritus of those last spoken: "No! I am in charge of my own destiny. I will not be the tool of you or your counselors. I refuse to marry for the sake of power. I am in love. Do you remember love, father? Do you? Love? You once had that for mother, but you've forgotten it since she's been gone."

Basia's face and form melted into a bright white, almost blinding, shining image of Selene. Her voice was soft, but increased in volume as she spoke. "Father. I love you. With all the affection of a loyal daughter for her father, I do. I love you." She smiled—her lips did not move as her voice made its annunciation—and as her smile grew, the whiteness that shone from her grew more and more intense as the volume of her voice increased until, at last, the

Judicar's sight was filled and he plunged face first into the water of the bath, blind save for the image of Selene seared onto his sight.

➢ Five ➣

Heterodymus sat opposite the Judicar as they jostled along in their pygmy-born carriage. Blinding spears of light frequently stabbed past the swaying, pitch-black window shades, due to the carriage's bumpy ride. On the outside, beneath the holocaustic sun, eight pygmies hefted the carriage on two long tree limbs thrust through massive metal rings on the coach's side. The couriers were outfitted with baggy white robes and cloth guantlets that matched the pure white of the carriage itself, wide-brimmed conical hats like inverted spinning tops, and round goggles with matte-black lenses that completely hid the eyes underneath, making their wearers look like four-limbed white insects from a distance. Horses would have been instantly blinded in such searing white light and, though they would have made the journey more quickly, the beasts could not have endured the trip as well as the pygmies, who had been bred for this very purpose, even retaining their eyes for navigation, unlike their blind palatial cousins. Beneath their flowing robes, their short, taut-muscled legs carried their human cargo with more fluidity than seemed possible for such squat creatures.

The Judicar donned his own pair of insectoid goggles to protect his eyes from the scalding sunlight before he cautiously peered out from behind the window shade. Heterodymus turned both heads away, holding up an arm for protection from the unbearable light that blared into the carriage, illuminating every interstice. The Judicar scanned the horizon to the south, spotting the distant gray peak of Mons Vinogradov, then let the curtain close. He removed the goggles, then pointed to a parchment map that sat on the table situated between them. The borders of Procellarium were outlined in white, making the nation look like some vast amoeba, sending pseudopodical roads out to several craters outlying the main body, stretching east to west from Crater Delisle to Crater Schiaparelli, and north to south from Angstrom and the Agricola Mountains to Bradley C and D. Euler lay straight east at a distance as wide as Procellarium itself, across a vast stretch of nothingness populated only by highwaymen and the hordes of foul creatures, both pets and scavengers, that attended them. It was for this reason that both the couriers and the carriage's passengers traveled well-armed.

The spots had just begun fading from Heterodymus' four eyes when the Judicar finally spoke. "We are making good time this eastward journey. Let's go over the situation in Euler while we have a moment."

Dexter looked up at the Judicar, then to Sinistrum, who rolled his eyes away to look at the carriage's roof. Finally, avoiding a return to the Judicar's inquisitive gaze, the younger head let his eyes rest on a pile of parchments that were resting on his lap. He thumbed through the series of documents as if he had not hear his liege's words. The Judicar was first simply annoyed by this strange behavior, then concerned as the thought struck him that Dexter did not wish to address the Euler issue.

Sinistrum, taking his brother's cue, and unable to distract himself with the hands that Dexter was using to collate documents, spoke to the perplexed Judicar, who dropped his head to the table to try to meet Dexter's averted gaze, half smiling, as if playing peek-a-boo with an angry child.

"Your majesty," Sinistrum began with a stern voice. The Judicar lifted his head to lock eyes with the left head of his counselor. His smile fell, and consternation showed on the ruler's face. Sinistrum continued: "Your majesty, Euler is not . . . particularly amiable to, nor aligned with our interests at the moment."

The Judicar shook his head, exasperated. He put his head in his hands.

"Not another war?" The scar tissue in his leg, only months old, throbbed at the thought. "My men need time to recover and train up replacements for those lost against the Scaramouche."

"Our agents see no military build up, sir," Sinistrum said.

"At least not directed against us," Dexter cut in, finally daring to look up from his papers at the Judicar's face. The ruler looked tired and batterfanged, Dexter thought, ready to suffer a nervous breakdown at any moment. Still the news must be broken. "They have," Dexter continued in his softest voice, "been sending more and more troops with their convoys, mostly Gruithuisen pikemen, supported by a smattering of Bessarion crossbowmen. Apparently they have been experiencing more raiding and convoy ambushes in the past several weeks than they have in decades."

"From what direction?"

"North," Sinistrum answered, the accusatory tone in his voice unmistakable.

The Judicar breathed deeply, a gloom setting in under his already-weary eyes.

"But," interjected Dexter, "the fault may not be entirely ours."

Sinistrum gave a condescending sneer to his body-brother: "Except that all of these raids and ambushes have been carried out by scattered bands of previously-pacifistic Scaramouche."

The Judicar looked at the map, focusing on the cartographer's skill and the fine scenes painted along its edges, in order to squelch the pang of sadness that flushed in his chest. He tapped the map, his finger landing on the precise spot of his daughter's grave. Recognizing the place, he quickly lifted his finger away, as if stung.

Sinistrum continued: "Euler feels that our battle against the Scaramouche has destabilized the region. They fear for the shipment of goods across the northern trade routes.

"Not that the Euler 'goods'," Dexter reinforced the sarcasm in his voice by creating quotation marks in the air with his upraised fingers, "aren't a destabilizing influence in and of themselves."

The heads began to bicker between them, but the

Judicar slowly raised his hand and his voice to stop the argument from developing further. Despite his frustration, he couldn't help but think how ridiculous the climax of an argument must be, should a two-headed being come to blows.

"Heterodymus. Heterodymus," the volume increased, "Heterodymus!" he yelled, startling them into silent attention. "You and I both know," he paused for a moment, thinking on the inadequacy of the word "both" to the situation, then continued, "what the records demand of us regarding the Scaramouche."

"Aye, M'lord," the heads replied in unison.

"Every eighth month, without fail or reprieve," said Sinistrum. The Judicar looked pained, his leg throbbing.

"At midnight," added Dexter.

"And you know," the ruler continued, "of our commitment to Euler, our eternal compact."

"Aye, M'lord," they both foresaw trouble.

"Then what is the problem? I mean to carry out our side of the old agreements, to the letter."

"To the letter, our Judicar," they resigned themselves to whatever might come to pass.

"Now, Dexter, recite again to me the doom of change. We will soon be drawing near to our destination."

The words clicked on in their mystical rhythm, a metronomic mnemon of ancient date, in lockstep with the slap of thick-skinned pygmy feet against hard-packed moon dust.

➤ Six ⤛

The sun was setting over the lunar horizon as they neared the borders of the Barony of Euler. For a few more moments it would shine like fire in the distance, then disappear in a wink, plunging the world into utter darkness, save where the blue planet lent its sun-borrowed glow.

Straddling the road that led from the south-western most inlet of Mare Imbrium was an immense archway built of light gray stones, each taller than a man standing on another man's shoulders. The arch itself was shallow, perhaps only forty feet at its highest point. And, if one dared challenge the guards who kept watch over the checkpoint that it marked, one could almost walk or ride a horse over the top of its two hundred foot length, as if it were a bridge. "Almost" because the structure was encrusted with tens of thousands of candles, of all different shapes and sizes, which melded into one gigantic flickering layer of flame. The archway, seen from a distance at night, mirrored the shape, if not the character, of the setting sun. This beacon, which served as the gateway to the Barony of Euler, could be seen for miles across the flat emptiness of the Mare. It was a welcome sight for weary travelers who had spent the day exposed to the danger of attack by the feral packs of creatures and bandits that stalked the uninhabited lands. Both Heterodymus and the Judicar let slip a slight smile—despite the seriousness of their visit—as they passed the guard contingent, who were dancing arm-in-arm, drinking from wineskins and singing bawdy songs of fighting and wenching. All of them, fifty or more, had woven flowers through the seams in their armor and ringed their heads with daisy chains. They turned to let the carriage pass through with a friendly wave before turning back to watch a group of dancing girls who gyrated suggestively to an unseen drummer's rhythms.

"So much for the stalwart keepers of the gate," Sinistrum hissed, laughing.

"It's all good fun," Dexter replied, also laughing. "You can't expect soldiers in such a stark place to always be alert."

The Judicar smiled and shook his head. "Yes, but odd. Very odd." His smile faded as his eyes narrowed with concern.

The remainder of the trip to Euler Crater proper was uneventful. The high walls, built along the circumference of the crater's rim, were well-protected by catapults, ballistrae, and archers who kept steady watch over the flats that led to the fortress. The carriage passengers prepared themselves for what ought to be a rigorous questioning of their business, even though it was apparent who was visiting and with whom he had business. Nevertheless, they expected to have to explain themselves as a matter of formality. The Procellarian guards would do the same to important visitors from Euler.

But the same sort of scene—only this time the soldiers were even more drunk—met them at the city gates. After a jocund hold-up, in which the guards teased, poked, and mocked the Judicar's pygmies, they were let through to meander through the twisting streets and intoxicated crowds of Euler until they finally disembarked from their coach at the palatial gates. The pygmies removed their goggles and hats, rushing to the nearest party, much to the locals' delight, by the crowd roar that received them. The city reeked of fermentation and the sickly sweet smell of lotus being smoked from many-hosed hookahs, like the insides of a school of octopus had been set on fire with dreams of stars and verdant paradises. The royal guards stumbled to let the pair inside the gates, a sergeant passing out on the threshold in the process. Two corpulent, under-dressed prostitutes lifted him off the ground and the gate shut behind the Judicar and his counselor with a bang.

Once inside, they were met by the court jester, the official emissary of the Baron and his Lady. She was short, nearly a dwarf, dressed in Harlequin black and white checkers: "A long and storied tradition," she noted brightly as they ascended a long spiral stairway past tapestry portraits of what must have been past jesters, judging by their ridiculous, yet evolving dress. "And an important part is mine. We have enough clowns here, as you, no doubt, saw at the gate. Those rapscallions, however, are amateurs, false dogs, dilettantes. My jest, however, is restrained, calculated, precise. Oh, the guards and the people alike take their jabs, but they do not understand the power of comical control. They are the masses, and I, their spiritual exemplar, though they are too drunk or too stupid to realize it. No doubt, our whole society is based on the balance, on one hand, of the people writhing in maenadic orgies of debauchery, their only concern the next intoxicant or orgasm, their only destination the music halls, the pubs, and the brothels. On the other hand are the Baron and his wife—circumspect, thoughtful, demure ...and downright boring. I am the bridge between the two, you see, the fulcrum on which rests the two opposing scales of order and chaos."

They came to a pair of immense oaken doors at the top of the stairwell. Painted on the door was a caricatured face, as tall as a man, of the Jester. The representation had been painted over several older portraits of past jesters. The paint was two inches think, in places, and the Judicar wondered how much history lay in those layers of paint, if only they could be peeled off one-by-one. The Jester turned to the pair, dwarfed by her own face behind her, and spoke in an artificially deepened voice, half sinister, half ridiculous, entirely deranged: "Come," her face grew dour, "My Lady awaits you."

The jongleur swung open the doors, then fell to her knees, crawling and barking like a dog. She rushed to the throne on which was sitting Lady Euler, the former Basia Pelevin, the Judicar's daughter. The fool sat up, begged, then pointed at the visitors, as if hunting pheasant.

"Begone, dog," commanded Lady Euler. The

jester rolled-over out of the chamber, stopping momentarily to scratch her back against the floor, then disappeared beyond the throne-room door, closing it shut behind her with her teeth.

Lady Euler stood up from her throne, a stately figure who wore her office well. Blonde hair cascaded down over the folds of her firelight-colored dress past the backs of her knees, in a golden cape. She was, by anybody's estimation, the most beautiful of the Judicar's daughters. But the Judicar saw little of beauty. Lady Euler's blue eyes pierced her father from beneath the diamond tiara that crested her brow. She pursed her full red lips and squinted malevolence at the Procellarian ruler. Her voice was ice:

"State your business."

Heterodymus stepped forward, bowed, then spoke. Dexter and Sinistrum's words were haunting, when spoken in unison, a kounterpunkt confluence of newborn and ancient, infant softness and geriatric croaking brought together as one voice:

"In token of the everlasting covenant betwixt our peoples, and beneath the blue planet that shines on both our fair regencies, we greet you, hailing you with multitudinous blessings, in purpose fixed to maintain peace and goodwill forevermore. These many generations we have enjoyed co-operation and mutual benefit by remaining good neighbors. Come, let us continue in our bond now and forevermore, rejoicing in one another's success, consoling each other in failure and sorrow, enfolded in friendship, eternally protected in togetherness, one always."

Heterodymus knelt, heads bowed before the Lady.

She stepped down from her dais and placed her hand on the twin's shoulder. "You, my friend, may be forgiven," she spoke slowly, clearly, as if every word she spoke was heavy with importance and difficult to bear, "for your offenses are not your own."

The bowed heads stole a look at each other, each a distorted mirror of the others puzzlement. No one had ever replied in such a manner to The Eternal Proposal. The ritual response, according to eons-old tradition, should have been "I wed thee, on behalf of my people, in an unbreakable bond." But this response was not forthcoming.

"No, Heterdodymus, you cannot be blamed for the Judicar's offense, for his breach of covenant." Puzzlement turned to astonishment on both of Heterodymus' faces. "Though you might suffer for his sins, it will not be at my hand. Arise, my old friend."

The Judicar watched as Heterodymus, horribly confused, was helped to his feet by Lady Euler – another breach of proper conduct.

"What madness is this?" the exasperated Judicar asked. "And where in hell is the Baron?"

"He will not be joining us," she raised her voice dramatically. "He has deferred this sour duty to me alone. I represent the Barony in this matter. And as to your accusations of madness, you shall soon see madness!"

She clapped her hands twice and from doors on either side of the room, a flood of drunken revelers entered, quickly filling the room with bodies, laughter, and a cacophony of voices. Music, wine-soaked breath, juggled pins, even the flaming explosions of fire-eaters filled the air, the carnival ruckus echoing off the chamber walls at an almost intolerable volume. The Judicar became dizzy with sensory overload. He spun to avoid the bumps and jostling of the dancing press, inadvertently joining the dance himself while trying to avoid it, caught up in the churn.

Heterodymus was doubly vexed by the movement and soon fell to one knee, overcome by a wave of nausea.

The Judicar briefly spotted his servant just as

Dexter, quickly followed by Sinistrum, disappeared beneath the perpetual vortex of bodies. He pushed toward the twin, indiscriminately groping arms, clothing, and clumps of hair in a desperate attempt to reach his advisor. He slipped in a pool of some liquid and was immediately plunged to the room's dark marble floor where he slid amongst a thick puddled mixture of beer, blood, wine, and other, less identifiable fluids. He tried to claw his way back up again, but the seeming hundreds of boots and sandals refused to let him stand. He looked up into a sea of legs that threatened to trample him like a vineyard grape into the slurry beneath. His breathing quickened as his fingers, arms, and legs were stepped on, sometimes intentionally stomped on. He suffered a battery of kicks, accidental and otherwise, to the ribs, face, and groin. Panic sounded a buzzing behind his eyes, a beehive of "Get out!" resonating in his skull. He went numb, vision temporarily blacking out as he made one last attempt to stand. He succeeded in getting to all fours, but was almost immediately thrust flat to his belly again with several feet to the back and neck.

A gong sounded—in his head? Or was it really the sound of a gong somewhere beyond the din of the deadly crowd? His ears had become unreliable because of the ringing that incessantly stung his drums.

Instantly, the noise subsided, like a candle-flame doused by an ocean wave. The voices grew somber, hushed, then completely silent. The revelers left the throne room without a sound, leaving footprints behind in a layer of mixed alcohol and bodily fluids as the only evidence of their passing. The Judicar was surprised to find Heterodymus, whom he thought incapacitated or worse, and helped the counselor to his feet. He leaned heavily on the twin, head still reeling. His knees nearly buckled as the doors once again opened in response to Lady Euler's hand clapping. Her face continued to show a stern, unemotional resolve.

The Procellarian pair braced themselves for another onslaught but were surprised when only a handful of figures emerged from the side doors, all except one with black stockings pulled over their heads to obfuscate their identities. The masked ones were the behavioral opposite of the crowd that had just left. They carried themselves with a grim air of circumspection and grave dignity. The Judicar recognized, with an audible shock, the lone un-masked member of the party—his own Assistant Deputy of Commerce. He was bound in iron manacles and leg chains. Two of the five hooded figures handled him roughly, pushing him to his knees on the slick floor, which caused him to tear leg muscles as he slipped in the muck. The deputy was terrified, eyes large with fear and body pained from the lashing he had received earlier, as evinced by the bloody stripes that showed beneath his tattered clothing.

"My liege!" the quaking deputy said in a trembling, pleading voice.

"Vadrich?" the Judicar asked with concern more than reassurance, then, turning to his daughter, "What is this?"

"The prisoner will answer. Speak well, mongrel."

The shaking deputy spoke in muted tones, deathly afraid to say the wrong words in the wrong manner.

"My liege, most high Judicar, after your departure for this place I was accosted in the basements of the ministry while searching for a set of records regarding our trading relationship with Marius C, the prince your daughter was to marry . . ." He stopped in mid-sentence, caught in the shock of what he had just spoken, suddenly realizing that he had crossed a boundary he ought not. From behind one of the black-hooded figures, the jester emerged, cart-wheeling between the Judicar and his deputy and chanting "Who's the fool now? Who's the real fool now?" The masked men showered brutality on the deputy, beating him with fists, feet, and knees, tearing at his hair, scratching his open wounds and kicking him repeatedly in the crotch until the Lady called "Halt!"

"Prisoner, continue . . . carefully," she ordered.

The deputy, winded and aching from the effort it now took to speak, obeyed, though every word was laced with pain.

"I was taken by an unknown hand and brought on horseback, with no protection for my eyes, to a darkened chamber where I was . . . questioned regarding the lotus trade." He looked at Lady Euler, trembling in the thought that he might have misspoken and offended her again. She simply smiled at him sweetly.

The Judicar turned to his daughter, utterly flabbergasted. "Is this true?"

Her smile dropped instantly and she turned to him. "He has said so. Do you not believe your own servant?"

"You vile bitch! What is so precious to you that you would jeopardize the relationship between our kingdoms? You selfish cur!"

She paused, again speaking carefully, with purpose.

"My father, the man I used to call 'father,' attempted to force my hand in marriage to Prince Marius C some years ago," the prisoner's eyes flitted to either side in anticipation of blows that did not fall, like a hare waiting for an owl to strike. "I refused, professing my love for Baron Euler. Then my father's wife died. She was no longer there to disappoint, and I thought that my father, being, up to that point, an innovator, might see the ridiculousness of the old ways and take the Baron as his own son. Instead, he embraced empty tradition and rejected me. So I married the man who accepted and loved me, the good Baron Euler. In time, my father finally received my oft-rejected entourage, but only begrudgingly, because tradition demanded it.

"Within the past few months, the Procellarian army, with the Judicar leading the charge, smashed the resolve of the people of Scaramouche by killing their leader, Cimbri Pelevin—the Judicar's own daughter, and my sister. Wandering bands of Scaramouche, now reduced to abject poverty since their delicate social structure was shattered by the casualties inflicted by the Procellarian knights, searched to and fro seeking sustenance and protection, or the means to attain such by force, if needs be.

"This disorder was introduced to the once-stable trade routes that covered the plains like a spider's web. Raiding parties spread from Rüinker Plateau north, across Sinus Roris, and southeast, across the Sharp-Marain foothills. This disruption has severely staunched the influx of the lotus flower to our kingdom, a kingdom whose very social structure depends on the balance between noble austerity and the hedonism of the masses. "Any fool," she pointed to the jongleur, who was sitting on her haunches like a begging dog, "can see that this threatens to destroy the barony from the bottom up." The Jester wagged her head up and down in agreement, slobber flying across her smiling face.

"You, Judicar Pelevin, have introduced chaos into our merchant's dealings, infecting our very bloodstream and upsetting the scales of social propriety. I will not see my people destroyed by your toyings with our commerce. You value order so highly. I think you will appreciate the removal of stochasticity from the system."

She nodded to the masked men.

"It is time."

The masked ones removed thin, black truncheons

from under their robes, then beat the deputy ruthlessly until his blood flowed freely, reddening the already slick floor under his slumped body. A few short convulsions later, the body ceased movement and was dragged out of the room by the snickering murderers to the cheers of a crowd that had been waiting outside. The jongleur cart-wheeled out behind them. The Judicar and Heterodymus could do naught but witness the murder.

Lady Euler strode up the few steps to her throne, then took her seat. She looked to the doors of the chamber, then quietly wept, careful to muffle her cries so that she would not be heard by those without.

"Father," she whispered in a sad tone of familiarity, the voice with which she spoke to him when she was a little girl, when they were both a little younger. He looked at her, shocked and unsure if he had heard her properly. "Father," the voice was genuine, "I am so sorry." She shook with sobs.

"It is a bit late for that," he said flatly. "How dare you order the death of my subject, before my very eyes. I swear I will have the records scoured for precedent to crush your precious Barony. I swear it and now, foresworn on my servant's blood, will not rescind the oath."

"But father, your deputy was only the scapegoat,

an effigy."

He glared at her, not understanding, confused.

"The merchant's guild—I told them that they must take out their bloodlust on the deputy . . ."

"Because they cannot get enough of their precious lotus?" he bellowed.

"No, father. I sacrificed your deputy to them because they wanted, instead, to kill you. And this will only forestall them for a little while."

"It shan't matter," he seethed, "I will never set foot in this place again."

"It does matter," she cried, frustrated at his lack of understanding. "You can't hide from the chain of events you set into play—only a part of those masked men were members of the merchant's guild. Some of those murderers were your own men."

⇢ Seven ⇠

Their ignominious departure from Euler was the antithesis of their stately arrival. The Judicar and Heterodymus left without an escort to find their carriage besotted with feces, rotting eggs, and vegetables. They gathered their drunken pygmies, some by the nape of the neck, and hitched them to their posts. When the Judicar opened the door to the carriage, the severed head of his Deputy of Commerce rolled out, a wide-eyed expression of horror rigor-mortified forever onto his palid face.

The carriage moved through Euler's winding streets, lolling and yawing with the inebriated stumbling of the portagers. The motion, combined with the sewer-stench of the layers that coated the vehicle's outside, gave the Judicar severe nausea. He vomited twice before they reached the city gates. The vehicle was pelted with rocks as they passed through the main portcullis, a cloud of bawdy insults ejecting them from the city. Sinistrum laughed despite himself at the creative suggestions for the use of their bodily orifices. Dexter shook his head in disgust at the crowd and his brother. The Judicar, dumbstruck, simply stared at the carriage floor, mute with shock.

After an hour or more of silence, Heterodymus lit the lanterns inside the carriage that would illuminate the dark-curtained carriage during their voyage home. The Judicar stared at the flames for what seemed an unhealthy, possibly blinding interval before he spoke.

"What can be done?"

Sinistrum, sensing his intent, spoke decisively, "Nothing!"

The Judicar turned to the other head, spots mingling with Dexter's face in the close press of the carriage-box. "He is right," the infant face spoke, his words registering in the Judicar's mind long after the mouth stopped moving. "Nothing is to be done."

"Our treaty is eternal, unchanging," Sinistrum concluded.

"I will find a way," the Judicar vowed.

"Is that wise, m'lord?" Dexter dared.

"Wise?"

"M'lord," Sinistrum snapped, "what of order?"

The Judicar looked into the flame again. "Order," he sighed. "Yes, order. You are right, my friend. Order."

The carriage tipped and swayed under the

immense blinding sun, the occasional black speck falling to the ground, picking itself up, and lifting its corner of the carriage again. A long, uncomfortable journey lay ahead for the occupants of the battered coach.

He was glad to be sitting in a stable chair after such a gut-wrenching journey. Hours after they had arrived home, the Judicar still felt the pitch and roll of the carriage. Although he was seated on his firmly-anchored throne, the room wheeled about him. Heterodymus and Selene appeared to shift and jitter before him. The nausea he had experienced in Euler remained unabated.

He finally focused his gaze on a trio of robed men sitting cross-legged on the floor. They were wizened old sages, surrounded by stacks of books and baskets overflowing with scrolls. They murmured amongst themselves, pointing to bits of text and arguing inconclusively about their meaning, drawing diagrams in order to explain their arguments to one another, emphasizing their systems of logic with hand movements that resembled the somatic component of some long-dead ritual.

Selene approached the throne, then, pointing to the three men, said, "Father, your lawyers are cunning, the best in the land." She smiled at him, but her face went sour as she turned to look at them. "But even they will not find what it is you are looking for. War with Euler is forbidden and has been so since the generation after Procellarium's founding."

Sinistrum and Dexter looked at each other with surprise, then nodded in affirmation to the Judicar, impressed by her knowledge of the nation's laws. They simultaneously looked at the Judicar with a touch of haughtiness, arms folded, heads cocked to the side, as if to say "You see? We told you so!"

"I suggest," Selene continued, "that rather than struggle with the letter of the law, which man cannot break—though they may break themselves against it—that we instead turn to the meaning of the Law of Sustaining, which is, that disorder must be recompensed with order." She walked about with an air of education, of astuteness, stunning the three lawyers with her confident demeanor. They looked up at her, unable to argue with her simple, yet profound logic.

The Judicar looked at his lawyers, who nodded to him that this was so.

"Your carriage, not to mention your deputy, came back in much disorder. This must be rectified or, rather, re-ordered. And those who caused the disorder must be made to fix the situation. If they cannot restore the life of your deputy, they must pay with their lives. The scales must be balanced."

Heterodymus unfolded his arms. Sinistrum's face showed astonishment, Dexter's suspicion.

Selene's tarans flew over from an unseen corner of the room, draping her in white ribbons as she continued.

"Therefore, father, use your recent victory over the Scaramouche to impose order on a region that has none. Station a group of your knights on the trade route between Euler and Scaramouche. Bring stability to that area and, while doing so, tax the merchants of Euler for their impetuosity. Tax them with their lives, if you see fit."

The lawyers nodded and smiled like a trio of entertained monkeys. Dexter rolled his eyes at their stupidity. Were it not for tradition, he knew, these men would have been involuntarily retired years ago for their senility.

"M'lord," he began to speak, but the Judicar held up a firm hand to silence his counselor.

"Let it be so. It is now decreed. Heterodymus, send twenty of my best men, along with their retinue, to secure the trade route. This should be sufficient."

"But M'lord . . ."

Again the upheld hand signified an order of silence.

The orders were fulfilled. Silence was maintained.

→ Eight ←

For weeks silence reigned over the palatial halls. It crept like a skittering wave of venomous black spiders into every crevice, the woolen weight of it only ruffled by the Judicar's sighs. Even the pygmy servants slowed their labors as they absorbed the growing malaise of their liege. The susurration of his murmurings made the air thick with brooding thoughts and malcontent. Such an air of darkness had not over-shadowed the throne room since the days of his wife's death. Disorder seemed to be percolating beneath the surface of it all, waiting for its chance to burst forth through the despairing veil.

Through this uneasy silence came the sharp-tapping footsteps of Heterodymus, who marched into the throne room. Selene stood behind her father, who was slouching on his throne, a half-empty chalice of wine in his hand. Sinistrum and Dexter stood silent before the Judicar, hands clasped behind the back. The Judicar had motioned for silence, and silence would not be broken by any but he who had decreed it. After an uncomfortably long time—too long even for patient Selene, who fidgeted with anticipation—he spoke.

"What news, Heterodymus?"

"None but ill," Sinistrum groaned.

"But it will please m'lord," Dexter sweetly intervened.

"Speak to me of Euler. The taxes, are they working?"

"All too well," Dexter said in a disappointed voice.

"You will be pleased to hear," Sinistrum's elocution was exquisite, words enunciated perfectly, but with a hint of being forced into formality, "that Euler has paid her debt for the dis-service that she has rendered. What might displease you is the dis-service that has been rendered Euler. She has been forced to beg food from her neighbors and has sold her crown for rags with which to cover her shame. She has wandered under frosting night and the withering sun of day. When her means were gone, she sold herself, her body and virtue, for mere morsels. Euler is a shell of her former self, but your oath remains intact. Law is still maintained between the two of you."

The Judicar smiled out of the corner of his mouth, as if he thought a joke was hidden in Heterodymus' comments.

"My dear Heterodymus, I have never known you to be so poetic. Your gift of allegory is remarkable."

"Allegory?" Dexter looked confused.

"Yes, your allegory about Euler and her sufferings. It is a beautiful, if a bit melancholy, metaphor."

"M'lord," Sinistrum began.

Dexter finished the thought. "Sinistrum's words, m'lord, were not metaphorical. We speak, quite literally, of your daughter, the Lady Euler."

Selene slowly walked out of the room, her tarans flitting behind her in the wake of the wind caused by her departure. The Judicar's face slackened at her departure and he croaked out a few un-intelligible words in an effort to speak.

"Lady Euler?"

"Yes, M'lord."

"But how do you know this?" The question came out haltingly, but with a hint of denial in its tone.

The reply was as smooth as Dexter's young skin: "She told us herself."

At this Heterodymus clapped his hands and a quartet of servants brought a stretcher through the pillars of the throne room. Two Procellarian knights chaperoned the injured occupant. She looked up, half-delirious, her blonde hair shining in the feeble light of the throne room, which had become darkened in more than mere spirit. Her robes had been torn to tatters and her bronze skin was peppered with black bruises and red scratches across her neck and arms. Teeth marks showed on her neck.

"Basia? You should not have come here." Sternness and compassion, even fatherly love, co-mingled in his voice. "You have condemned yourself by coming here."

She whispered feebly. "I know that father," a tear carved down her dusty face. "But my death is inevitable. My people have rejected me and debased my body—I could not maintain order as they wanted or needed."

"Order? There is only chaos in Euler," he said angrily.

"Order on the trade routes. I could not maintain it. But this is of no consequence."

"The consequence of coming here under decree of banishment is death...I cannot stay the law," the last phrase carried strong tones of resentment.

"It does not matter. I came here to die, but only after I saw you one last time."

The guards motioned to the servants that they should pick up the stretcher and follow them.

Heterodymus—both Dexter and Sinistrum— looked at the Judicar with pleading expressions.

The Judicar looked at his chalice. "I cannot stay the law," then, after drinking its sweet contents, he let the metal vessel clatter to the floor, dented, scuffed, his tears spilling from its mouth onto the throne room floor.

⇢ Nine ⇠

The Judicar sat on his throne, brooding in near-darkness. He had not eaten for days. Only the draughts that Selene brought to him from time to time sustained him, quenching his thirst and giving moisture to his filthy skin. The only movements he made were the laborious trips to the cistern and to bed, to relieve himself and catch a few hours of troubled, unsatisfying sleep. Selene helped him, as he was sometimes so weak that he was unable to hold himself upright. In those moments, he thought of her as an angel, her white hair shining through his dolor.

She stood behind his throne as Heterodymus entered the room only long enough only to make a short, almost-mechanical announcement before wheeling about and promptly leaving. "It is done." The Judicar, even in his weakened state, could see that his servant was merely following procedure in the most perfunctory manner possible. He raised his hand to the twin's receding back, trying to hail him, but Selene gently pushed the hand back down to the arm of the throne while giving the retreating counselor an icy stare.

"Father, you should not worry so about Heterodymus."

"But he is my friend and my counselor."

"No, father. He is merely a servant." The tarans were sleeping in the air above her, cradled in hammocks of silk scarves.

The Judicar's voice filled with sadness. "He is disappointed in me."

"He does not understand your accomplish-ments, father."

"Accomplishments?" he said in surprise. "Accomplishments." He chuckled, then coughed. "Tell me of these accomplishments, my dear Selene." His voice was a touch slow, his words slurred from lack of sleep. He looked ten years older than when he had first gone out to battle against Cimbri and the Scaramouche.

"Your charge against the Scaramouche was most brave," she said cheerfully.

"Brave?"

"Yes, you rode gallantly into the enemy, though severely outnumbered. And all the courtiers and their daughters commented at length on how handsome you look in your armor." She smiled and winked at him.

"Bah! True men of war do not care for fashion in battle. What do women know of such things?"

"Not nearly enough, I suppose. But beyond fashion, you charged headlong into the midst of an opposing force . . ."

"I became lost," he laughed in self-deprecation.

"...and bested their leader in one-on-one combat."

The Judicar abruptly stopped laughing.

"And now, father, you have defeated another enemy, snatching victory from ignominy without even the use of arms." She pounded her fist into her hand with each of the last six words for emphasis.

She knelt next to his throne, looking up at his downcast face from the arm of the throne. His blue eyes were empty of light, reflecting pools of heartache.

"And you did this without breaking your oaths. You have unflinchingly kept your side of every covenant you have entered. Is not this a thing of great merit? Lesser men would have buckled under your pressures."

She stood up before him, holding his hand in hers. He looked up at her softly-glowing whiteness. "And, most importantly, you have restored order to

Procellarium and righted the wrongs of entropy. For this you shall be hailed for generations to come as the last Judicar worthy of his title."

He looked down at his lap again, then up at Selene. He stood suddenly, decisively, startling the napping tarans awake. They rubbed their eyes with tiny fists, then looked at him with disdain through half-open lids.

"You are right, my dear. I have fulfilled my imperative and must continue to do so. My spirits have flagged as of late, but I see now that I have discharged my duty well." He slowly bent his back, then sagged down into his throne.

"But still?" Selene questioned, sensing that he had something more to say.

"But still . . . I am saddened."

"I think, my dear father, that you suffer from being locked away in your chambers for so long. You have forgotten about the common people to whom you have dedicated your time and efforts. By all means, you should be joyful in their presence, father. You are allowed discretion, in certain matters of ceremony, to do just that. Some pomp might do you good. A parade, perhaps?" She smiled.

An odd thing, thought the Judicar, that he had never, ever noticed her smiling before this conversation. Not in all his years.

A grin expanded across his face. "Yes. Yes, I deserve – my people deserve a bit of celebration."

He snapped his fingers, bringing several waist-high pygmy servants scampering in to fulfill his orders.

"This will be a celebration to remember!" Selene exclaimed. The Judicar was invigorated. A new energy permeated the palace. Light had returned.

⇸ Ten ⇷

The Judicar welcomed the publicity of the parades. Events of state were the one time the Judicar did not feel quarantined from the rest of common society. Most of the year was spent insulated from the majority of the population by his knights, his counselor and, possibly, lawyers, his servants, and his family. Even during times when affairs were going well, being before the public was like fresh air, a patch of green grass in the lunar desert. Today, for the first time in a long time, he would feel alive again.

They stood on a broad balcony—the Judicar, Heterodymus, Selene, and a group of a dozen bodyguards and servants—a hundred feet above the street. The balustrade was richly cut with ivory geese, necks and wings intertwining in an architectural ballet along the railing's edges. The archway behind them was crested with a pair of geese, wings extended to hold up the keystone—a delicately carved white marble frieze of the blue planet above. Buildings across the promenade blocked the harsh light of the setting sun, allowing the company reprieve in their immense rectangular shadows. Above them the main palatial tower thrust into the sky, stabbing its minaret top a thousand feet or more into the evening light. If one looked too long at the borders of the buildings across from them, one would see their rectangular shapes burned onto their vision for some time to follow.

On the street below marched the Knights of Procellarium, at the head of a long parade. Few knights could be spared due to the security issues to the north, but those in attendance were resplendent in silver, holding long poles. On the top of each pole was attached a shimmering orb that cast a soft phosphorescent white glow over the streets and walls, a lesser light to rule the night. Behind them marched the less-heavily armored, but no less beautifully-attired militia. Since these men were only to be called upon in times of great need, their dress was more ceremonial than functional, as the laws and covenants of Procellarium were created to discourage incidents that might require a full-fledged army to resolve them. Their helms were, in keeping with the décor of the kingdom, geese whose wings covered the wearer's face, save where splayed feathers allowed eyeholes. The crest was the goose's own neck and head, thrusting up and forward from the back of the helmet in a threatening, open-billed pose. Each man wore a white tunic with a small black cravat at the neck, white cape, gloves, and boots, the last two items flared dramatically at mid-arm and calf.

The militia was several thousand strong and looked like a river of undulating milk, above which bobbed their spears and standards. The people on the sidewalks and alleys below scrambled to see the spectacle while the sounds of a band of drums, trumpets, and bagpipes grew stronger behind the militia.

The people. The Judicar had all but forgotten the magnitude of his responsibility, how many thousands relied on him to keep order. His knights, the largest group with which he would, indeed could, surround himself for any length of time, was a speck in the ocean when compared to the throng that was his nation. He was weighed down with the thought of caring for so many people, the power of ruler-ship drowned out by the charge of leadership. He felt small and alone, the magnificent shouts of the crowd silenced by the roar of responsibility in his head.

He waved perfunctorily. Selene smiled and waved to the crowd, beaming from their attention, feeding on it. The Judicar looked at her and was glad for her happiness, hoping only that she might find more and more of it. He had no other daughters left to bless.

But Selene's smile abruptly ceased, and the shouts of the crowd came back to the Judicar, only this time in a cacophony, the chanted lauding of Procellarium's leader and laws turned to screams and random shouts of anger and fear. He looked down to see a small group of citizens fighting with the militia, as if a stone had rolled off the bank and into the river of milk. Several knights wedged their way through the crowd to the source of the disturbance, sending a wave through the throng.

Most of the malefactors were contained by the combined efforts of the knights, militia, and a majority of the crowd. But a few individuals and small groups slinked through the morass of bodies and made their way through the dark and empty streets of the city beyond the parade route. A group of militia detached from the main ranks to take the prisoners to a nearby square where they would surely be punished by summary execution for crimes of disorder, as the laws dictated. Some of the crowd followed, drawn on by morbid curiosity, but most of the people stayed to watch the parade resume some semblance of normalcy, the stone worn down by the river, though pieces flushed through beyond it and back onto the bank, waiting for the opportunity to once again cast ripples in the stream.

As the last of the crowds dispersed into the streets, the Judicar walked through the archway and through a series of winding hallways to the throne room. Selene took her leave and the royal bodyguards took their posts at the doorway as the Judicar sat down on his throne. Heterodymus stood silent before the throne for an uncomfortably long time, watching the Judicar. But his lord only sat, thinking. He started several times, as if to speak, but each opening word was caught in the net of a conflicting thought before it could be fully released from his mouth. Heterodymus continued to stare at him, patiently waiting.

"What disturbs you, Heterodymus?" he finally asked. "You may speak freely."

The voices, both Dexter's and Sinistrum's, came so quickly that the Judicar had difficulty determining which was which. At times one would begin a sentence, while the other would end it. He had never heard this cross-pollination of sentences before and was nearly hypnotized by the effect.

"You saw the crowd,"

"the disturbance . . ."

"Rebellion is being fomented."

"It is being allowed from within."

The Judicar sat upright. "Are you accusing...?"

"You?"

"No, but our laws prevent such a thing from happening."

"Unless . . ."

"Unless the laws are not being enforced."

The Judicar shook his head, dizzy and confused. "Then who?"

Dexter and Sinistrum looked hesitant, as if wanting to avoid the very subject that they had brought up.

"It is difficult to bring such accusations before you."

"Such accusations carry consequences, whether they are proven true or false, m'lord."

The Judicar stood and screamed in frustration, fists coming down on both thighs in a rage. "Speak, damn you! If you know something, then out with it, now!"

The twins looked at each other, resignation showing on both of their faces.

The Judicar regained his composure, sitting back down on his throne with a sigh. "Heterodymus, speak. You are my counselor, and what you say here need not go further."

They looked at each other, Sinistrum and Dexter, and nodded to each other as if to assuage their mutual fears and assure their support for one another, brothers to the end.

"You have heard the crowd, m'lord."

"How they chanted."

The Judicar chuckled, "But they always chant at such occasions. 'Hail the Judicar, may our nation never fail,' and 'To order, to order, we ardor for order,' blah, blah, blah. It is all pre-programmed, just as the traditions require."

The twins have him a surprised, nearly shocked look.

"Sir. Did you hear their exact words today?"

"It's all a murmur from the balcony, Heterodymus, and with the cloud that has hung over me, my senses are dulled." He put his hands up to his head, massaging his temples.

"M'lord, after chanting momentarily to your long health,"

"they began a new chant."

"A new chant?" The Judicar rose from his throne and walked to a window across the chamber, his steps slowing as the twins stated in eerie unison:

"Queen Selene, Queen Selene, Queen Selene."

The Judicar stood at the window, peeking out into the night. He wondered for a moment, how many had been put to death at the gallows since the disturbances, then looked up at the stars that peppered the night with their astral flares. After a moment, he turned to his counselor.

"Honestly, I see no harm in this. The girl will, in time, be Queen, there is no doubt. By rule of law, she will marry a fit young man and assume her role as Queen and comforter to the next Judicar. What is the harm in her being recognized as the future wife of he who will hold the throne—whomever that might be?"

Heterodymus said nothing, but produced a scroll from the folds of his garments. He handed it to the Judicar, who cautiously slipped the ribbon from around its circumference, then unrolled it before a candle, letting the flame illuminate the thin parchment behind the dark ink of the words:

Requisition all knights to the southern borders of Schiaparelli crater, minimal militia guard to replace knights patrolling Sinus Roris—Euler corridor. All engagements with Scaramouche, bandits, and Euler personnel are to be avoided. Effective immediately. No authority shall supercede this order unless I personally approve it.

Selene Pelevin
Heir Apparent

⇢ Eleven ⇠

A tall, thick-chested guard entered the throne room, striding past Heterodymus as if the counselor did not exist. The guard looked straight ahead, his gaze falling on the wall above and behind the Judicar's throne, careful not to look the ruler in the eye. He proclaimed: "M'lord, an ambassador from the north declares his desire to enter your royal presence."

The Judicar sat up straight in his throne. "His request shall be granted," then, after a split second of hesitation, "Guard, stay with us."

"As you wish, sir," the guard's sight remained fixed on the wall behind the throne until he wheeled towards the pillars at the front of the throne room. "Pre-sent the ambassador!" he barked to the guards in the hallway.

A dark figure wove a winding path through the pillars. Its fine features were hidden in shadow, but the silhouette was un-mistakable. A sound of whispers and rustling leaves hissed from the tall figure, though only the outline of its immense nose and the voice's location beneath the impossibly tall top hat indicated where a mouth might exist.

The Scaramouche Ambassador stepped out from the shadows, obviously shy of the low light flickering from torches along the walls. Its face, underneath the mask, was a flat black blank, as of a human wearing a black silk mask, without eye, nose, or mouth holes. The proboscopic mask was made of ivory and painted with vine-like indigo symbols around the eyeholes and along the snout—a detail the Judicar had missed in his melee engagements, the only intercourse he had previously had with them being at a sword's length or more and that in churning dust. The figure wore a black tuxedo over black tights and knee-length black leather boots. He—had the guard not said "he"? — carried in . . . his hand a large leather bag, the type that a medical doctor would carry his instruments in while doing house calls. No clatter of metal came from the bag. As his eyes carved over the figure, the Judicar realized that this was the first time he had seen a Scaramouche outside of combat. They were, indeed, beautiful, if terrible, the sheer calm-ness of their demeanor their most disturbing aspect.

Giddiness entered the Judicar's head as the ambassador spoke, an uninvited feeling as of slight drunkenness.

"Father of Cimbri," sorrow hit the Judicar at the mention of her name. "I come to bring ill tidings from my people, who you, in your ignorance, call the Scaramouche."

The guard tensed, putting both hands on his as-yet upright pole-arm. The Judicar shifted in his chair, ready to spring, if necessary.

"We have maintained peace for many years, fully aware that your pre-destined forays into our lands would take some of our numbers from us. Until recently, it was considered an honor for those of our kind to sacrifice themselves on behalf of, and for the preservation of, the larger population. This was done regularly, on each of your military excursions in years past, as a token of the individual's willingness to give all for the common good, and to maintain peace and prosperity within our lands.

"But now these sacrifices bring us shame. For rather than being satisfied with fulfilling their ritual obligations to the state, your knights exact taxes where, before, the very idea of taxation was anathema. Rather than a mere ceremonial raid, your knights have ransacked our villages, slain our women and children indiscriminately, and without provocation. Your interference with the black lotus trade is unprecedented and irrevocably catastrophic to the fabric of our society. Were it not for our trade with Euler, we should surely be completely destitute. We hold a delicate position in the Sinus Roris as it is, our lives precariously hanging over the edge of a precipice each day.

"My people are slipping into the abyss, and they cry out for vengeance on most quarters, though a few—very few—pacifists remain. But all, regardless of their ethical position, suffer for lack of sustenance. In their desperation, they have turned on one another in violence, a thing that has never happened in our society before. Never. It tears at the very seams of our identity, our sociality, and all that we teach our sons and daughters, whom we love.

"And thus for love, for the sake of our children and our love for them, we, at this moment, formally declare war on the Procellarian nation."

The Judicar looked up at him, the hint of a smirk on his face. But the ambassador spoke before he could give a reply.

"A light shows in your face. Hope, I presume, that you will easily do away with this annoyance. Hope not, Judicar Parmour Pelevin, for our ceremonial encounters in the past have been just that. We have thrown a shroud over the true might of our arms for some time. At our leader's command, a sea of black will lap against the walls of Procellarium. Our forces will climb the bodies of your dead like ladders, to surge over your defenses and through your bedroom windows and fill your streets with sorrow. We will infect your vision with a new view of chaos. Your light will soon be extinguished. I take my leave."

The ambassador strode toward the exit, then stopped, turned, and reached into his bag. "Oh, and a friend of mine asked me to deliver this. A gift from a friend of my people."

The guard instantly lowered his pole-arm and moved into attack position, but the Judicar held up his hand, staying what would have been a swift execution.

From the bag the Scaramouche gently lifted a round object that crackled dryly as he threw it to the ground at the Judicar's feet. It took several moments for the Judicar to recognize the mummified head of his Deputy of Commerce, which had earlier rolled from the royal carriage on the Judicar's and Heterodymus' departure—no, evacuation—from Euler.

Heterodymus, stifling his gag reflex, reached down and carefully removed a note, which was attached to the head by a long pin through its dessicated, wormlike tongue. He rolled the note open as the Scaramouche departed into the hallway, to be escorted back to the northern borders.

Sinistrum read:

The joke is on you, Judy. The Baron and Lady are merrily rotting and things have become so topsy-turvy here that now I, the mountbank, am in charge. Imagine that! A fool ruling a country. But you should understand that quite well. Oh, but we are having a grand time of it. Even the merchants have joined in on the shenanigans. Have I mentioned that things here are really upside down? We're celebrating here in the tower, but the common folk have gone dour. They're all serious—deadly serious. They want so badly to see your head in the same state as your deputy here, they've decided to press your borders with Euler. Let them have their fun, says I! It's been nice knowing you.

Hugs and kisses and tons of well wishes,

The Jongleur Euler

After a pause, Dexter spoke. "This does not bode well. Ill tidings indeed."

The Judicar sat in a deep distress, fighting to

maintain his composure. In short order, the impossibility of his position restored his boldness. Determination reanimated his demeanor, clarity and decisiveness reclaimed his mind.

"Countermand Selene's order immediately. Send out our swiftest messengers with this command: All knights and militia that have headed south will immediately change course and return here. Furthermore, send all the knights and militia in the city to hold off the Scaramouche to the north, the mobs of Euler to the east. Then command Selene to visit me here in my throne room."

A tittering laugh sounded from among the pillars, filled with childlike glee. A mocking voice called out, "Oh, but father. You are too late on both accounts— the army," Selene spun around a pillar into view, her lithe form echoing the curves of the pillars, "and me!" The tarans chuckled overhead, holding their hands to their mouths to keep their laughter from bursting out across the chamber. Their ice blue eyes peeped out over their hands and down at the Judicar with a maladorous glee.

✤ Twelve ✤

Up and up they climbed above the highest of the palatial buildings, up even above the lip of the crater in which the city rested, a spiral stairway ascending the highest hollow to a point unreachable by all save the royal geese that slept a thousand feet below in a shadowy corner of the Judicar's lush garden, barely visible by the naked eye. At the top of the stairs a door, and hanging on a wall near the door several pairs of blackened goggles that they donned—the Judicar, his daughter, his counselor.

Sunlight haloed the door like a corona as it opened on to a circular gazebo—a dazzling white latticework cupola laced through with vines and leaves of all shades of green. Three doorways opened out on to balconies that looked out over the lunar landscape—the most spectacular view of or on the moon. The blue planet hung suspended close overhead. The Judicar thought that if he could but jump high enough, he could grasp hold and be taken around the globe of the moon, hanging from the blue-green orb as if from a balloon.

The shadow of the blue planet partially eclipsed the sun, casting an ever-growing shadow over the white sands. To the north and east, campfires burned from the city gates all the way back to the curve of the moon, covering the horizon. To the southeast a tiny whiff of horse-hoof-driven dust heralded the imminent arrival of the Judicar's re-assigned knights and militia. It was clear from this aerie that the Procellarian forces would be snuffed from existence in a matter of minutes, should they be so foolhardy as to charge the combined Scaramouche-Euler army. The horrisonant clatter of rioters wafted up from the city streets below and small fires erupted from windows and doorways in every quarter. Even the smaller buildings of the palatial compound had begun to take flame. The faint stench of smoke could be smelled even at this dizzying height.

"So," Dexter spoke in his falsetto baby voice. "You've done it," Sinistrum scratched out the conclusion to the enigmatic sentence.

The Judicar turned to his counselors. He cocked his eyes sideways in puzzlement. If the trio could only see beyond the jet blackness of each other's protective goggles they would have noted the confusion in his gaze. "Done what?" he demanded, confused.

Selene looked out over the encroaching armies, her smile growing with each new campfire, each puff of smoke and flame beneath, each progressing mile of darkness cast down by the waxing eclipse.

Heterodymus' voices blended as one, both twins speaking in exact mimesis of the other in word, tone, fluctuation, as if their brains had finally fused into one entity, young and old become mature, optimist and pessimist turned pragmatist, left and right turned to center.

"Light is dawning on me even as the darkness falls. Her sister's unfit ends used to her own. Their cessation of life and power further her own ambitions to rule and live as Queen of Procellarium, beautiful and terrible, her father cast down from the throne not only by enemies from without, but, primarily, by his own hand. An intrigue with the Scaramouche and Euler, and the quiet urging of rebellion against the old order of the Judicar to bring in the new order of The Queen. This world, M'lord, can never be the same. I fear that this is the end of your rule."

The Judicar turned to his smiling daughter. "Is this dark congress true? This secret combination of darkness and treachery?"

She giggled teasingly. "Almost. I will tell the rest in a moment, but, yes, Heterodymus is right about many things. Not the least of which is the removal of the old regime to create room in which to usher in the new. Therefore, I see no need for the old counselors. I have my own twins."

The tarans, who had kept still to this point, swooped down, a bundle of scarves swinging between them. They caught Heterodymus in a tangle of white lace, a silk and satin web, which they dragged, laughing, into the air and cast into the city streets below, Heterodymus' billowing flailings and shrieks were lost as he plummeted to the screaming farrago beneath—a city enveloped in blankets of black smoke and flame.

The Judicar fell to his knees and looked up again at the tarans, who innocently played with the train of Selene's dress, as if their infant minds were incapable of understanding the murder they had just committed.

"And I suppose they shall kill me next," he said resignedly.

A pained expression crossed her face and she clicked her tongue while shaking her head, as if simultaneously chiding and feeling pity for an ignorant child.

"No, no, Daddy. How could I let that happen? It would be . . . improper for me not to complete the chain of events I set into motion those many, many years ago when I was but a child."

The Judicar blinked behind his goggles, as if trying to force a vision from the past into being before his eyes. His confusion grew.

"I . . . I try to remember you as a child, but I have no recollection of you being other than what you appear to be right now. You have always appeared thus, for as long as my memory serves me. How many years?"

"Oh, surely I can't be expected to remember the exact number of years, but I suppose you do. Back when I realized that you were too weak to rule effectively, despite your best efforts. Back when I tried to accelerate your growth into the responsibility of ruler-ship—a responsibility that I now see you cannot uphold. Back when I pushed that pillar as the gong sounded in the royal gardens, late, late at night."

"You?" he stood, dumbfounded. "Y . . . you!" A hint of fight swelled up within him, welling up through the sadness that threatened to crush his heart. He fled from that scene in the mind's eye past to root himself in the present, where he could make a stand on more stable mental ground. It was an amazing emotional feat, a victory of sorts, and he felt a slow returning of his strength and will.

"And what now is stopping me, Selene, from casting you to the ground from this place?"

She reached into the folds of her dress and drew out two small scrolls. "Only a pair of agreements. One between me and the leaders of the Scaramouche that I will establish friendly, peaceful relations with them and help them rebuild their shattered infrastructure, and one between me and Euler that I will not only allow free interchange and trade, but that the Knights of Procellarium will protect all trade routes between Euler, the Scaramouche, and our glorious nation. Agreements not with Procellarium, mind you, but with me personally."

He looked out over the almost completely black surface of the moon, a tiny wedge of light about to disappear on the northeastern horizon.

"Then the die is cast."

"Not quite," Selene admitted, her honesty catching him off guard. "I suppose you could kill me out of spite or revenge, but it will do you little good. The poisons I have slowly been administering to you over several years in your drinks are almost ready to take their final hold. You might live long enough to see Procellarium fall into total anarchy and the opposing armies infest what remains of the city and its people, spreading slaughter and rapine in their wake. Or," she held out a vial of black liquid, "you can die honorably, at your own hand, assured that I will maintain order in the kingdom. A lasting order that shall not ossify and become arthritic with outdated tradition, as the old order has."

He considered for a moment, then took the vial with a trembling hand. He looked at her, wishing he could see her eyes through her goggles, to read her true expression. Then, as quickly as he could, he quaffed the vial's contents. The strength of the contents knocked him immediately to the floor, the world swirling about in a vortical blur of color and texture, as if everything were filled with, and exuded, a prismatic spray.

The shadow of the blue planet fell completely. Selene removed her goggles, as the sun, behind the hills, could not now blind her, and she wanted him to see her face as he lay dying. She looked at her father as he pushed himself up to his hands and knees and removed his goggles. Through the chromatic whirlwind he saw her face – saw it more clearly than he ever had before, as if his past views of her had been through a distorting glass that had now been removed. Her countenance shone, an iridescent aura enveloping her white hair, casting lambent rainbows into the churning prism-vortex.

A glimmer of revelation sparked in his eyes, then a full-fledged sun broke over his clouded mental horizons. "I know now," he wheezed his last, failing breaths. "You are not alive, you are dead."

She laughed, an honest laugh, not malicious, like the sounding of a million tiny silver cymbals.

"Father—how silly you are! Did mother not tell you of her pregnancy before the fall? How can that die, which was never born?"

Selene, Queen Selene, reached down to close his eyelids. The vortex dissipated, along with her beautiful face—the face of one never born, never alive, never dead, everlastingly never—into the void.

About the Author

Forrest Aguirre is a recent recipient of the World Fantasy Award for his editing of *Leviathan 3*. His fiction has appeared in *Flesh & Blood*, *American Letters & Commentary*, *Prague Literary Review*, *Redsine*, *3rd Bed*, *Notre Dame Review*, *Exquisite Corpse*, *The Journal of Experimental Fiction* and *Polyphony*.

Forrest is the editor of the new experimental fiction anthology series *TEXT:Ur* from Raw Dog Screaming Press. He is co-editor (with Deborah Layne) of an anthology of women's fiction titled *The Nine Muses* from Wheatland Press.

Locus Magazine calls Forrest, "...an interesting writer, worth watching, whom I think could benefit from disciplining the wilder flights of his imagination a bit." Forrest spurns such disciplinary measures.

A collection of his short fiction titled *Fugue XXIX* was published by Raw Dog Screaming Press in 2005. *Swans Over the Moon* is his first novel.

Forrest lives in Madison, Wisconsin with his family.